WIN OR LOSE

BY JAKE MADDOX

ILLUSTRATED BY SEAN TIFFANY

text by Eric Stevens

STONE ARCH BOOKS
a capstone imprint

Impact Books are published by Stone Arch Books
A Capstone Imprint
151 Good Counsel Drive, P.O. Box 669
Mankato, Minnesota 56002
www.capstonepub.com

Printed in the United States of America in Stevens Point, Wisconsin.
092009
005619WZS10

Library of Congress Cataloging-in-Publication data is available on the Library
of Congress website.

Library Binding: 978-1-4342-1919-0
Paperback: 978-1-4342-2281-7

CREATIVE DIRECTOR: Heather Kindseth
ART DIRECTOR: Kay Fraser
GRAPHIC DESIGNER: Hilary Wacholz
PRODUCTION SPECIALIST: Michelle Biedscheid

TABLE OF CONTENTS

Team JAKE MADDOX

WILLY WILDCAT, COACH T, TREY, DANIEL, DWAYNE, ISAAC, PJ

#		Position	PPG	FT %	FG %	Stl
	Danny Powell	Center	9	73.2	82.8	5
11	Daniel Friedland	Forward	5.7	95.8	85.1	12
13	PJ Harris	Center	22	65.6	90.2	7
23	Trey Smith Ⓒ	Guard	14	96.2	80.5	20
26	Isaac Roth	Guard	11.5	94.1	79.3	11
33	Dwayne Illy	Forward	6.2	82.9	77.9	9

Athlete Highlight: **PJ Harris**

PJ Harris is the first string center for the Westfield Wildcats. At 5'10, he is the tallest member of the team. PJ is known for his defensive skills and his layup abilities. His weakness is his free throws.

Chapter 1
JUST PRACTICE

PJ Harris looked down at his shoes, size 13. He was the tallest guy on the Wildcats basketball team, and his feet were the longest. But he wasn't thinking about his feet, or his height. He was thinking about the foul line.

He looked up. The basket hung ten feet high, thirteen feet away. Down both sides of the lane, players stood in red or yellow jerseys, watching him out of the corners of their eyes as they looked up at the basket.

PJ looked down at his yellow jersey, then at the ball, and took a deep breath. His heart was pounding. He could hear the voices of people watching, cheering him on or taunting him.

He looked up at the basket, pulled the ball back over his shoulder with both hands, and shot.

Brick!

The whole backboard shook as the ball slammed into the rim, then fell right back to the wood. It bounced hard into the lane, and one of PJ's opponents grabbed the rebound. In seconds, it was back up the court, and the other team had scored.

A whistle blew and PJ shook his head. "Scrimmage over," the coach called out. "Red jerseys win."

It was only practice, but PJ felt awful. "Man, why can't I ever make a foul shot?" he muttered to himself.

Dwayne Illy, the starting small forward, heard him. "What did you say?" he asked.

PJ turned and said, "Oh, nothing. No big deal. I missed the foul shot. It's just practice, right?" He laughed and gave Dwayne a high five.

"Practice is where we improve, PJ," Coach Turnbull said. "If you'd stop goofing around when you miss those foul shots, maybe you'd improve."

"I know, Coach T," PJ replied. "I'm not goofing around."

I'm only laughing so I don't look stupid, he thought, but he didn't want to explain that to Coach Turnbull.

"Don't even worry about it," Dwayne said. "Who cares about a center shooting foul shots?"

"Yeah, that's your job," PJ said, smiling. "You take most of the foul shots, 'cause you get fouled a lot."

"That's right," Dwayne said. "And I have the best foul shot on this team. So no worries, right?"

PJ laughed. "How many foul shots do I even take a season?" he said. "Like four?"

Dwayne nodded. "Maybe two!" he said. The two boys laughed and joined the rest of the team for layup drills.

Chapter 2
AGAINST THE JAGUARS

The next day was Thursday — game day. The Westfield Middle School Wildcats took on the Grayson City Jaguars.

Since PJ was the tallest player on the team, he went to the center of the court for the jump ball. The referee tossed the ball up and PJ jumped. With his fingertips, he knocked the ball toward Dwayne.

The Westfield side of the stands cheered. PJ was feeling good.

He ran with his team up the court and took his spot at the bottom of the lane. The other team's center was guarding him very closely. *Too closely*, PJ thought.

The Jaguars center elbowed PJ as he moved across the baseline.

"Watch it," PJ said. He used his arm to box out the other player when Trey Smith, the Wildcats shooting guard, put up a three-point attempt.

The shot missed, but PJ jumped up. He grabbed the rebound and laid it back up for two points.

"Nice job, Harris," Coach Turnbull called out. He clapped a couple of times. "Way to get in there. Keep boxing that guy out!"

PJ ran up the court and picked up the other center on defense.

When the Jaguars small forward moved down the lane, faked a shot, and tossed the ball to the center, PJ was right there. He put up a hand and easily blocked the layup.

The Jaguars center fell on his butt in the paint. The ref blew his whistle to stop play.

PJ tried to help the other player up. "Hey, man," PJ said, "sorry about that."

But the Jaguars center just smacked his hand away. "I'm fine," he snapped. He got to his feet.

It was a tight first half, and PJ worked hard for every rebound. He blocked a couple more shots — including two more layup attempts by the Jaguars center.

When the buzzer sounded, the Wildcats were up by only two points. PJ watched as the Jaguars center stormed off the court.

Chapter 3
PLAY HARD

Right before the start of the second half, Coach Turnbull stood in front of his team's bench. The players were all seated or standing around.

"Great job in the first half, guys," the coach said. "Dwayne, how are you feeling? Up for starting the second half?"

"I feel great, Coach T," Dwayne replied. "Man, I could play these fools into the ground all day." He laughed.

"I know it," the coach said. "Same five, then. Huddle up."

The five starters stood around the coach and leaned in.

"On three, 'Wildcats,'" the coach said. "One, two, three . . ."

And the five starters shouted: "Wildcats!"

The huddle broke, and the guys took the court.

"Just a second, Harris," Coach Turnbull said.

PJ turned and jogged back to the coach. "Don't you want me in again, Coach?"

The coach nodded. "Of course," he said. "Your hustle is great today. You're really giving that Jaguars center a hard time."

"Thanks, Coach T," PJ said.

"Just be careful. Don't be too rough," the coach added. "I don't want you to get in trouble out there."

PJ nodded. "You got it, Coach," he said. Then he went to the sideline.

The ref blew his whistle, then handed the Jaguars center the ball. The Jaguars center threw it in to one of his teammates. No matter what PJ did, he couldn't reach the ball.

The fans in the visitor bleachers cheered. PJ shook his head and ran up the court. He picked up his man at the baseline and tried to keep him out of rebound position.

The Jaguars shooting guard took a shot from just inside the three-point line, and it swished. No rebound required. The game was tied.

The second half was tiring. PJ's man was playing very hard and very rough.

While PJ played, he watched his teammates. Each of them was playing his hardest. Every point they scored was fought for, and every drive they stopped was even tougher.

As the clock ticked down, the score stayed painfully close. With only a few seconds left on the clock, the Wildcats were down by one point.

Isaac Roth, a Wildcats point guard, held the ball for an instant at the top of the key. PJ stepped in front of his defender and cut hard under the basket.

It was just enough time for Isaac to connect with PJ, who caught the pass on the way up to the basket.

Suddenly he felt a strong arm across his throat and shoulders. The next thing he knew, the ball was bouncing slowly toward the bleachers, and his butt was on the wood.

A whistle blew. "That's two," the ref shouted.

PJ looked up at the scoreboard. The Wildcats were still down by one, and he had two chances to tie it up, or even win.

Chapter 4
CHOKE

PJ stood at the foul line. He held the ball under one arm and looked up at the basket. His hands were sweaty. PJ wasn't sure if it was from the tough game, or his nervousness.

Coach Turnbull called out from the bench, "You got these, Harris. We only need one for the tie."

"Come on, PJ!" the players called from the bench.

A hand slapped his back. "All you, Harris," Dwayne said from behind him.

In front of PJ, Wildcats and Jaguars lined up, waiting for his shot.

From the bleachers, he heard classmates shouting, "PJ! PJ! PJ!"

From the other side, some students from Grayson City called out, too. "Boo! Choke!"

PJ tried to ignore them, but his heart pounded and his hands shook. Finally he looked up at the basket, pulled back his arms, and shot.

Right away, he knew it was an air ball. The ball arced too soon and dropped at least six inches short of the rim.

The ref handed the ball back to him for his second shot.

"That's okay," the coach called out, clapping. "You've got another shot, and we only need one point to enter overtime."

PJ's mouth felt dry. He squinted through the sweat in his eyes, drew back the ball, and shot.

This time it wasn't even close. The ball slammed into the backboard and dropped right into the hands of the Jaguars power forward. He grabbed the ball, drove it quickly up the court, right past Dwayne, and laid it up for another two points. Then the buzzer went off.

The ref blew his whistle. He called out, "Game over."

PJ looked at the gym ceiling and shook his head. He muttered to himself, "Life over."

Chapter 5
LEAST POPULAR

When Friday morning's alarm buzzed next to PJ's head, he groaned.

"Up and at 'em, PJ," his dad called from the kitchen.

But PJ was all out of energy that morning, and not just because the game the night before had left him exhausted. He also knew he'd have to face an entire school's worth of angry people.

He had blown the game against Grayson City Middle School, and everyone knew it. He wouldn't be surprised if the principal mentioned it on the morning announcements during homeroom, just in case anyone had missed the game.

"Come on, Peter Joseph," Dad called, more sternly. "Unless you want to walk in the rain, you better move. I have to leave for the shop in fifteen minutes, and you're not skipping breakfast."

PJ got to his feet and rubbed his eyes. Then he got dressed in the clothes he thought would attract the least attention. Of course, when you're fourteen years old, but five feet and ten inches tall, people notice you no matter what you wear.

PJ walked into the kitchen. "Morning," he mumbled.

"Why the long face?" Dad asked.

"I blew the game last night," PJ said. "Because of me and my awful foul shots, we lost to Grayson City."

Dad frowned. "Ouch," he said. "They're one of Westfield's biggest rivals."

"No kidding," PJ said sadly.

"I doubt it was really your fault," Dad said. "There are five guys on the court at a time, right? They all made a difference, win or lose."

PJ shook his head. "You don't understand," he said. He went to the fridge and took a swig of OJ from the carton.

"I'm pretending I didn't see that because you're in a bad mood," Dad said. "Eat fast. You have ten minutes."

At school, PJ kept his head down. There was no announcement about PJ blowing the game, of course, but they did announce the final score. A few people in PJ's homeroom, including Dwayne, glared at him during the announcement.

PJ dropped his head onto his desk. He kept his head on his desk until the buzzer rang and everyone else left.

When he picked his head up, Dwayne was standing next to him.

"Oh, uh," PJ stammered. "Hi, Dwayne."

"I can't believe you showed your face today," Dwayne said.

PJ leaned back in his chair and looked up at the ceiling. He sighed. "It wasn't all my fault we lost, you know," he mumbled.

"Oh really?" Dwayne said. "Was someone else up at that foul line shooting bricks and air balls?"

"We all played the game, Dwayne," PJ replied. "If you had scored more baskets during regulation play, we would have won. Maybe it was your fault."

"What?" Dwayne snapped.

PJ shrugged. "I'm just saying," he said. "I'm not trying to blame you."

Dwayne took a deep breath. "All right," he said. "However you want to break it down, PJ, the whole school is mad at you right now."

"I know," PJ said. "I was thinking about asking for your help."

"You want some tips on shooting free throws?" Dwayne asked.

PJ nodded. "Big time," he said. "I need all the help I can get."

Dwayne looked at the clock. "You sure do," he said. "But right now I need to get to class or Mr. Fishman is going to mark me absent and give me another detention."

"After school," PJ said. "Meet me at the outside court?"

Dwayne nodded. "Yeah, all right," he said, backing out of the room. "I'll see you, PJ. Keep your head down today."

PJ heard him laughing as he walked away.

Chapter 6
LESSONS?

As PJ pushed through the back doors of the school that afternoon, he could feel the other students' stares like laser beams. But then he heard the rubber echo of a basketball not far off, and he felt a little better.

PJ went around to the north side of the school. There was Dwayne, dribbling the basketball, and sinking shots from the outside.

Dwayne looked up and saw PJ, then did some trick dribbling, drove on the hoop, and laid it up smooth.

"Nice one," PJ said, walking up.

"Yeah," Dwayne replied. He took the ball up to the free-throw line. "Now, first lesson. Watch the master."

PJ went over to the baseline and stood under the backboard. Dwayne stood at the line, pulled the ball back over his shoulder, and in one smooth motion took the shot. It was perfect.

PJ caught the ball off one bounce. He started heading to the free-throw line.

"Not yet, PJ," Dwayne said, holding his hands out. "Toss it back."

PJ stopped in the key and shrugged. "All right," he said. He passed the ball back.

"You need to study my form a little more," Dwayne explained. He looked up at the basket and let another shot fly. It went in off the backboard.

This time, the rebound rolled back to Dwayne. He scooped up the ball and lined up another shot.

PJ stood at the baseline and watched as Dwayne took shot after shot. Every time PJ got a rebound, Dwayne told him to give the ball to him one more time.

"Hey, Dwayne," PJ said. "Think maybe I should take a few shots if I want to get any better?"

Dwayne hushed him and took another perfect foul shot. "I think for your first lesson," he said, "you should just watch the master."

PJ waved him off. "Man, I've seen you shoot about a thousand free throws before I came out here today," he said.

Dwayne laughed and took another shot. "And you still can't shoot," he said. "So you better keep watching."

PJ shook his head. "This is ridiculous," he muttered. Then he walked off toward the bus stop.

Dwayne called after him, "You'll never learn!"

PJ mumbled under his breath, "Not from you, anyway."

Chapter 7
PRACTICE!

Monday couldn't have come soon enough. Normally PJ loved the weekends, but he didn't want to see any of his friends from the team, since they all probably still hated him. And he couldn't go down to the park courts to practice because it rained Saturday morning to Sunday night.

Early Monday morning, PJ walked down the quiet halls of Westfield Middle School toward Coach Turnbull's office.

The office door stood open, so PJ reached in and knocked on it. "Hey, Coach T?" he said nervously.

"Oh, Harris," Coach Turnbull said. He was sitting as his desk, sipping coffee out of a mug that said *I Love Dogs.* "Come on in."

"Do you hate me as much as the rest of the team does, Coach T?" PJ asked. He sat down in a chair.

The coach put down his mug. "Hate you?" he asked. "What are you talking about, Harris?"

"You know," PJ replied. He didn't look the coach in the eye. "Because I lost the game for us on Thursday."

"Lost the game?" the coach said. "That's crazy. You missed a couple of foul shots. Lots of guys missed shots."

PJ shrugged. "I guess," he said.

"Listen, Harris," the coach went on, "you didn't lose the game for us, but you should work on your foul shot. Why don't you talk to Dwayne? He's got a great free throw."

"I don't think so," PJ said. "Any other ideas?"

"Well, there's Daniel Friedland," the coach said. He looked through some papers on his clipboard. "His foul shot has really improved over the last season. I think he's gunning for the starting five at Dwayne's position."

PJ thought about it. He had noticed Daniel's shots improving a lot, even though he hardly ever played in a game. "Okay, Coach," PJ said, getting up. "I'll find Daniel and ask for some tips."

"I'm glad you're trying to improve that shot, PJ," the coach said.

* * *

Daniel Friedland was in PJ's math class. PJ went over to him just before class started.

"Hey, PJ," Daniel replied. "Bummer about that game last week, huh?"

"I'll say," PJ said. "At least you're speaking to me."

"I don't think anyone's mad at you about it," Daniel said. "At least not anymore."

PJ said, "I was hoping you could give me some tips. I know your free throw has gotten a lot better since last season."

"You noticed that?" Daniel said excitedly.

"Sure," PJ replied. "So did Coach T. He said I should ask you for some tips."

Daniel beamed. "Wow," he said. He got a faraway look on his face. "You think Coach T will let me start soon?"

"Come on, Daniel, focus," PJ said. "How did you get better?"

Daniel looked at PJ. "Huh?" he said. "Oh! Right. Well, I just practice. A lot! Like, every morning before school, I spend thirty minutes at the park courts, just shooting foul shot after foul shot."

PJ's eyes opened wide. "Every morning?" he said. "That's insane. What time do you get up every day?"

Daniel shrugged. "Six. It's no big deal," he explained. "My mom makes me breakfast and I head to the park."

The bell rang to start class, so PJ slid into his seat at the back of the room.

Every morning? he thought. *And at six? That's so early. I don't know if I can do that.*

* * *

The next morning, PJ's alarm went off at six. Somehow, he managed to pull himself out of bed. He threw on some sweats and a hoodie, then some socks he found that didn't seem too dirty.

"What are you doing up already?" his dad said when PJ reached the front door.

"I'm going to shoot some free throws at the park," PJ said. He pulled on his basketball shoes. "I need to improve my shot if I don't want to lose any more games for the Wildcats."

When PJ made it to the park courts, the first thing he saw was Daniel Friedland, shooting from the foul line.

"Hey, you made it," Daniel called out. "Nice."

PJ said, "I guess I'll use the other basket."

Daniel nodded, then went right back to shooting free throws.

Man, he's so serious about it, PJ thought. Then he went to the other basket and stood at the foul line.

PJ yawned. He glanced at his watch. It was only six thirty. School wouldn't start for another hour and a half.

That leaves plenty of time to practice, he thought. *If I can stay awake.*

PJ glanced over at Daniel. He wasn't as good as Dwayne from the line, but he was sinking most of his shots.

PJ looked back at his own basket, then at his ball. He took a deep breath, spun the ball between his palms, and lifted it up.

He aimed. And all he could think about was Daniel, behind him, watching him.

PJ took another deep breath, drew the ball back, and shot.

Brick.

The ball slammed into the metal rim with a thud, shaking the backboard and the pole. Then it bounced right back at him, over his head, and onto Daniel's side of the court.

"Aw, man!" PJ shouted.

Daniel caught PJ's ball and tossed it back. "No big deal," he said. "Keep going."

PJ glared at Daniel, who smiled and went back to practicing. PJ stood, facing his own basket, listening to the sounds behind him: the ball bouncing once or twice. Then silence. Then the ball hitting the rim and falling in, or hitting the backboard and falling in. Then the ball would bounce another couple of times and PJ would hear Daniel's feet on the cement.

PJ's heart raced. The sun was behind his hoop, and he squinted toward the basket. After a deep breath, he bounced the ball once, lifted it up, and shot.

The ball came off his fingers all wrong. There was no arc, and no power. It fell at least six inches short of the front of the rim and rolled onto the grass.

"No!" PJ shouted. Then he walked off.

"PJ?" Daniel called after him. "What about your ball? PJ?"

But PJ ignored him. He had one option left, and that was to quit the team.

Chapter 8
QUITTER

PJ still had an hour before school started, so he decided to head home and have breakfast.

Then he'd go to school, find Coach T, and quit the basketball team.

"Back already?" PJ's dad asked when PJ walked into their apartment. "You can't have gotten much practicing done."

"It was a waste of time," PJ said.

He kept moving right through the living room, down the hall, and into his bedroom. There, he flopped onto his bed.

Dad followed him. "What's going on?" he asked.

"I'm going to quit the basketball team," PJ said. Then he picked up a stuffed mini basketball from his bed and shot it at the trashcan across the room. It went in.

"Quitting the team?" Dad repeated, shocked.

"Don't get mad," PJ said. "I can't shoot a foul shot to save my life. All I'm good for is being tall."

"That's nonsense," Dad said. "You're great at getting those rebounds, and I've seen your shot. It's good! And you love basketball!"

"My shot is good?" PJ said. "You should have seen me this morning at the courts. A brick and an airball. It was a really great show. Daniel Friedland is probably still down there, rolling on the cement with laughter."

"I doubt that," Dad replied. "What was he doing down there at this hour anyway?"

PJ explained how Daniel had gotten so much better this season by practicing early every morning.

As he talked, he got up from the bed and grabbed the stuffed basketball out of the trash. Then he sat down on the bed's edge again and shot the ball again. Again, it went in.

"So maybe you should do the same as him," Dad suggested.

"That was my plan," PJ said, "but with Daniel right there, I got so nervous."

"Because Daniel might be watching you?" Dad asked. He sat next to PJ on the edge of the bed.

PJ shrugged. "I guess," he said. "I don't know what to do about it. My heart races, I can't take a deep breath, and my hands sweat. Plus, now the whole team hates me, which makes it even worse!"

"I get nervous too," Dad said. "At the shop, I sometimes get so frustrated when I can't get a cut just right, or when I start assembling pieces and the whole shop is noisy and I can't concentrate."

"Dad, basketball and carpentry have nothing to do with each other," PJ said, rolling his eyes.

"Just hear me out," Dad said. "When the shop is like that, and I just can't think straight, and the piece isn't coming together like I need it to, sometimes I just want to take whatever I'm working on and throw it at the wall. Just forget about it."

"So do you?" PJ asked.

Dad smiled at PJ. "No way. I can't do that," Dad said.

"Why not?" PJ asked.

"Well," Dad explained, "because this is for some customer who needs his new dining room table, or kitchen cabinets, or whatever. So I take a deep breath, and I close my eyes. And in my mind I picture the pieces going together perfectly. I go over the whole thing in my head, so everything fits just like I measured it."

"And?" PJ said.

"And before you know it," Dad said, smiling, "I can't even hear the other guys in the shop. The machines are quiet, like they're miles away. I take a deep, calm breath, and get back to work. Then it always works out."

PJ lay back on the bed and thought about what his father had said. Maybe he was right.

Maybe they both got nervous. Maybe the same thing that worked for Dad would work for PJ.

Chapter 9
GAME DAY

PJ didn't quit the basketball team when he got to school on Tuesday, but during practice that afternoon, he wished he had. He managed to sink a couple of shots, but he still felt really nervous with everyone watching him.

When game day came around on Thursday, he was sure the coach would keep him benched. But he was wrong. He started, like he always did.

"Are you sure, Coach T?" PJ asked as the other four starters got on the court. "I've been choking a lot."

"I'm sure," the coach said. "Get out there, okay?"

PJ shrugged and went to center court for the jump ball.

The ref blew his whistle, then tossed the ball up. PJ was much taller than the center from East Harrington, and he won the jump easily. He got his whole hand on the ball and knocked it right to Isaac, the point guard. Then he ran up the court and took his place at the bottom of the key.

Isaac held up two fingers on his right hand, then cut to his left. PJ knew that meant he would look for Dwayne at the top of the key.

PJ moved to the top of the lane to set up a pick just as Dwayne caught the pass and started to drive toward the hoop. PJ stood right in the way of Dwayne's defender and Dwayne made the layup easily. The score was 2-0, Wildcats.

The whole first half went well. PJ got a lot of rebounds, and scored eight points from the floor. When the second half started, the Wildcats were up by ten points.

In the second half, PJ quickly got the ball. He passed it to Isaac, but then everything started going wrong.

Isaac tried to find Dwayne when he cut across the key, but the pass was blocked. When the East Harrington player started driving quickly back down the court, Isaac chased him on defense.

Under the Wildcats basket, Isaac jumped to try to block the East Harrington player's layup, but he didn't reach it. Instead he landed on his side, out of bounds. The coach and the school nurse ran over to him.

"It's not serious," the nurse said, "but it will be a nasty bruise. He should sit out the rest of the game."

The coach sighed and waved to the bench. The second-string point guard would have to play.

From then on, the Wildcats really had to struggle. PJ worked hard under the boards and got a few rebounds, but several plays fell apart. The second-string point guard didn't know them as well, and his passes weren't quite as smooth as Isaac's usually were.

With only a few seconds left, the Wildcats were down by one point. Dwayne Illy took a hard drive through three defenders. The ball got knocked out of his hand, and right into PJ's, under the basket.

PJ pumped once, then jumped up and tried to lay the ball in. But two defenders came down on his arm and knocked him to the wood.

The whistle blew.

PJ's heart nearly stopped. His team was down by one, and he was about to go to the line. Again!

Chapter 10
AT THE LINE

PJ was sweating. He pulled his wrist across his eyes to wipe away some sweat, then looked up at the game clock. There was less than one second left.

The defenders and PJ's teammates were lined up on both sides of the lane. All of them watched him.

The ref handed him the basketball, and PJ spun it between his palms.

PJ looked at his teammates. Dwayne looked at the floor and shook his head. Isaac Roth, with a wrap on his knee, sighed and looked away. Daniel Friedland tried to smile, but he looked nervous. Trey Smith, their captain, winked at PJ, but didn't smile.

Coach Turnbull clapped and shouted, "You can do this, Harris. We only need one to tie. We can win it in OT!"

PJ looked up at the stands. His dad was in the back row of the bleachers. He looked right at PJ, then closed his eyes, and smiled.

PJ shrugged. It was a worth a try. So he closed his eyes.

In his mind, he pictured himself shooting. The ball left his hands smoothly and sailed perfectly toward the basket.

It felt right coming off his fingers. In his mind, it was a perfect swish.

After a few seconds, PJ couldn't hear the coach, or the cheering and booing from the bleachers. It was as if he was completely alone in the gym.

PJ held the ball in his hands and lifted it up to aim. Then he opened his eyes. He felt himself smiling, and he shot.

Swish!

The whole gym went crazy. Everyone from Westfield jumped at the same time. The other Wildcats leaped up from the bench and cheered for PJ.

Coach Turnbull shouted, "Great shot, Harris! You tied it up. No pressure at all now. Just take a nice shot. Either way, we got these guys in OT!"

PJ looked at the coach and nodded, then looked at his dad and smiled. His dad gave him a thumbs-up.

PJ looked back at the basket. This time it was easy. He closed his eyes a moment, took a deep breath, and shot.

Off the backboard, the ball dropped for the second point.

As the ball fell through the hoop and bounced onto the wood, the Wildcats players and their fans jumped up again. They swarmed the court, cheering for PJ.

PJ couldn't believe it. The Wildcats had won!

"I guess watching me shoot really helped, huh?" Dwayne Illy said.

PJ rolled his eyes.

"Did you find a different court to practice that shot on?" Daniel Friedland asked. "I haven't seen you at the park since Tuesday morning."

PJ laughed and shook his head. "Nope," he explained. "I had it in me all along. I just didn't know it till my dad showed me where it was."

THE AUTHOR
ERIC STEVENS

15

ERIC STEVENS LIVES IN ST. PAUL, MINNESOTA WITH HIS WIFE, DOG, AND SON. HE IS STUDYING TO BECOME A TEACHER. SOME OF HIS FAVORITE THINGS INCLUDE PIZZA AND VIDEO GAMES. SOME OF HIS LEAST FAVORITE THINGS INCLUDE OLIVES AND SHOVELING SNOW.

24

THE ILLUSTRATOR
SEAN TIFFANY

WHEN SEAN TIFFANY WAS GROWING UP, HE LIVED ON A SMALL ISLAND OFF THE COAST OF MAINE. EVERY DAY UNTIL HE GRADUATED FROM HIGH SCHOOL, HE HAD TO TAKE A BOAT TO GET TO SCHOOL! SEAN HAS A PET CACTUS NAMED JIM.

GLOSSARY

arc (ARK)—a curved line

attempt (uh-TEMPT)—try

exhausted (eg-ZAWST-id)—very tired

huddle (HUHD-uhl)—to crowd together in a tight group

opponents (uh-POH-nuhnts)—the people playing against you in a game

option (OP-shuhn)—something you can choose to do

referee (ref-uh-REE)—someone who supervises a sports match to make sure the rules are followed

rival (RYE-vuhl)—someone you're competing with

scrimmage (SKRIM-ij)—a game played for practice

DISCUSSION QUESTIONS

1. PJ has a hard time with free throws. When you're having a hard time doing something, what are some ways to get better?

2. Who helped PJ the most in this book? Discuss your answer.

3. Why do you think PJ wanted to quit the team?

WRITING PROMPTS

1. Write about a time you had a hard time doing something. Who helped you? How did you get better?

2. Do you belong to a team? Write a few sentences about the other members of your team.

3. What would have happened if PJ had quit the team? Write about it.

MORE ABOUT CENTERS

In this book, PJ Harris is the center for the Westfield Wildcats. Check out these quick facts about centers.

* The center is usually the tallest member of the team.

* A center's job is to score and defend the basket.

* In the NBA, a center is usually nearly seven feet tall.

* Because they're tall, the centers are usually the people who take the jump ball at the beginning of the game.

* Famous centers have included Kareem Abdul Jabbar, Wilt Chamberlain, Shaquille O'Neal, Dikembe Mutombo, Will Perdue, Chris Webber, Patrick Ewing, and Yao Ming.

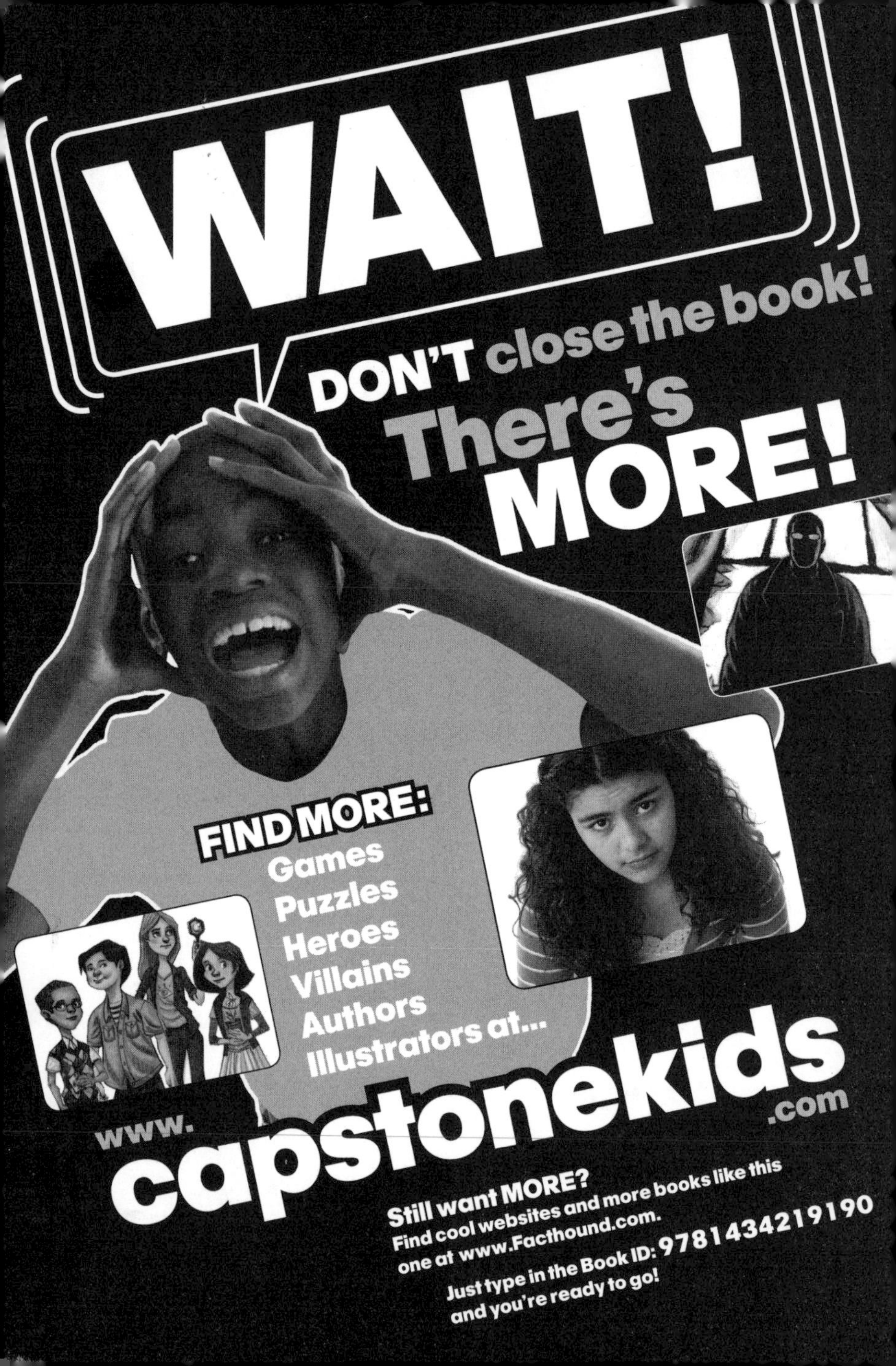
WAIT!
DON'T close the book!
There's MORE!
FIND MORE:
Games
Puzzles
Heroes
Villains
Authors
Illustrators at...
www.
capstonekids
.com
Still want MORE?
Find cool websites and more books like this one at www.Facthound.com.
Just type in the Book ID: 9781434219190
and you're ready to go!